W9-ADZ-013

Police

Risa Brown

Bethany, Missouri

Photo Credits:
Cover © Tony Tremblay; Title Page © Frances Twitty; Page 4 © Christophe Testi; Pages 5, 12 © MalibuBooks;
Page 7 © Soubrette; Pages 8, 11 © Frances Twitty; Page 9 © Jim Parkin; Page 13 © Paul Gardner,
Ronald Bloom: Page 14 © Michelle Malven; Page 15 © Jan Tyler, Timothy Hughes; Page 16 © Jason Osborne;
Page 17 © Joel Terrell; Page 18, 20, 21 © Jan Tyler; Page 19 © Anita Elder: Page 22 © Tony Tremblay

Cataloging-in-Publication Data

Brown, Risa W.
Police / Risa Brown. — 1st ed.
p. cm. — (Community helpers)

Includes bibliographical references and index.
Summary: Text and photographs introduce what police
officers do, where they work, and things they use in their jobs.
ISBN-13: 978-1-4242-1357-3 (lib. bdg. : alk. paper)
ISBN-10: 1-4242-1357-6 (lib. bdg. : alk. paper)
ISBN-13: 978-1-4242-1447-1 (pbk. : alk. paper)
ISBN-10: 1-4242-1447-5 (pbk. : alk. paper)

1. Police—Juvenile literature. 2. Police—United States—Juvenile literature.
3. Police—Vocational guidance—Juvenile literature. [1. Police.
2. Police—Vocational guidance. 3. Occupations.] I. Brown, Risa W.
II. Title. III. Series.
HV7922.B76 2007
363.2'2—dc22

First edition

802 N. 41st Street, P.O. Box 505
Bethany, MO 64424, U.S.A.
Printed in China
Library of Congress Control Number: 2006940998

Table of Contents

Keeping You Safe

Police officers want you to be safe. They work all over your city or town.

NYPD
POLICE
POLICE

Police Station

Police officers begin their **shift** at the police station. They learn where they will go that day. They learn about any problems in their area.

Patrol

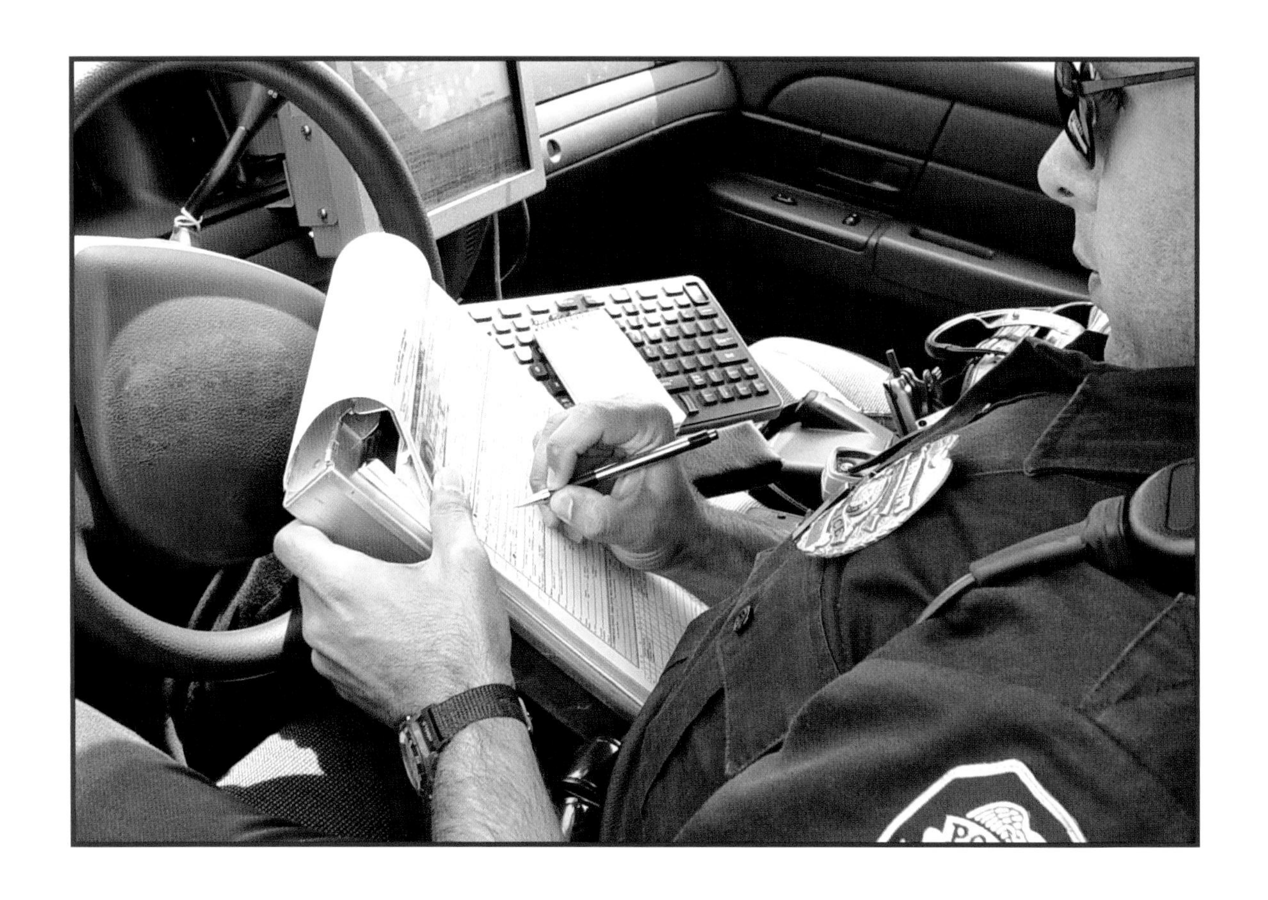

Some police officers **patrol** in police cars. They write a ticket if someone drives too fast.

They will help you if you get lost or get in trouble.

Arrest

Police officers **arrest** anyone who breaks the **law**. This can be **dangerous**.

Uniforms

Most police officers wear a uniform, a badge, and a hat. They may wear a **bulletproof vest** for **protection**.

Bulletproof Vest

Badge

Equipment

Police officers always have a radio and **handcuffs**. They may also have a gun and a club.

Club

Getting Around

Some police officers patrol their neighborhoods by walking.

Some ride bicycles or motorcycles.

Some police officers ride horses during outdoor events such as a parade.

Some patrol in boats.

Police Dogs

Some police officers work with dogs. The dogs are trained to chase **criminals** or find things that have been hidden.

Staying Safe

Police officers help people everywhere to stay safe. If you need help, look for a police officer.

Glossary

arrest (a REST) — to catch and hold someone who is breaking the law

bulletproof vest (BUL it pruf VEST) — a vest that keeps bullets from hurting an officer

criminal (KRIM e nel) — a person who is breaking the law

dangerous (DAN jer es) — doing something that is not safe

handcuffs (HAND kufs) — two steel rings that lock together so that a person cannot use his hands

law (LAW) — a rule made by a country or city that everyone must follow

patrol (pe TROL) — to go around an area to watch for trouble

protection (pro TEC shun) — to keep something or someone safe

shift (SHIFT) — the time when a police officer works

Index

FURTHER READING

Bryan, Nichol. *Police Officers.* Abdo, 2003.
Gorman, Jacqueline Laks. *Police Officer*. Weekly Reader Early Learning Library, 2003.
Lowenstein, Felicia. *What Does a Police Officer Do?* Enslow, 2005.

WEBSITES TO VISIT

Because Internet links change so often, Fitzgerald Books has developed an online list of websites related to the subject of this book. This site is updated regularly. Please use this link to access the list: www.fitzgeraldbookslinks.com/ch/pol

ABOUT THE AUTHOR

Risa Brown was a librarian for twenty years before becoming a full-time writer. Now living in Dallas, she grew up in Midland, Texas, President George W. Bush's hometown.